I wish I could... SLEEP!

A story about being brave

Tiziana Bendall-Brunello

Illustrated by John Bendall-Brunello

QED Publishing

Little Bear was trying to go to sleep when he heard a strange screeching sound.

Little Bear felt a bit scared.

"Oooooh!" he said to himself. "I wonder what that was?"

Little Bear peered round
the edge of the cave.

"Hello, Little Bear!" said Owl.
"What are you doing out here?"

"Well, I heard a scary sound
coming from the tree..."
replied Little Bear.

"That was only ME!" said Owl.

"I wish I could sleep,"
yawned Little Bear.

"Why don't you try my bed?" suggested Owl.

Without another thought Little Bear climbed into Owl's nest.

He tried to make himself comfortable.

He wriggled a bit.

He turned a bit.

But just then...

CRACK!

And Little Bear started to fall.

"Ooohhhh!"
called Little Bear.

Luckily Little Bear fell right into a big pile of leaves.
"Now I really do want to go home to MY bed,"
he sighed.

But he was suddenly startled by something rustling in the leaves beside him.
"Ooooooh!" Little Bear froze.

"Hello, Little Bear!" said Raccoon. "What are you doing here?"

"Ahh, it's you," said Little Bear. "I just want to go back to my bed. I wish I could sleep."

"I need to collect more leaves to make my bed warm and cosy," said Raccoon. "But you can try sleeping in my bed."

But try as he might, Little Bear could only just get his nose down the hole.

"Oooh, I just want to go home," wailed Little Bear.

So off he went... but just then he saw a
strange shadow moving slowly across the path.
"Oooooh!" cried Little Bear. "What's that? It looks like a..."

"Hello, Little Bear!" said Moose gently. "Don't be afraid. It's only me. What are you doing out here?"

"I couldn't sleep, but now I just want to go back to my bed," said Little Bear.

"Jump up here then – I'll give you a ride!" said Moose.

"Now try to think of happy things to help you go to sleep. That's what I do!"

In no time at all, Little Bear
was fast asleep.

"What a brave Little Bear you are!" whispered Moose softly. "Night, night!"

Notes for parents and teachers

- Look at the front cover of the book together. Ask the children to name the animal. Can the children guess how the animal feels?

- Ask the children what happens at night. Can they see the Moon? Can they see any stars? What do they do before they go to bed? Do they wash, brush their teeth and give their mum or dad a big goodnight kiss? Do they take their teddy bear to bed?

- Can the children name all the animals in the book? Ask them which animal they like the most and why.

- Talk about the leaves, including their size, colour and shape. You could ask the children to collect different sizes of leaves and stick them onto a sheet of white paper.

- There are many things that Little Bear is afraid of. Discuss with the children what these are and why. What do you think made Little Bear afraid of the moose? Discuss why Little Bear should not be afraid of a moose, despite the difference in their size.

- Ask the children if they have problems with their sleeping like Little Bear. Discuss what makes people sleep well. Discuss why it is important to have a good night's sleep.

- Ask the children to draw a picture of themselves sleeping, together with all the things that make them sleep well.

Consultant: Cecilia A. Essau
Professor of Developmental Psychopathology
Director of the Centre for Applied Research and
Assessment in Child and Adolescent Wellbeing,
Roehampton University, London

Editor: Jane Walker
Designer: Fiona Hajée

Copyright © QED Publishing 2011

First published in the UK in 2011 by
QED Publishing
A Quarto Group Company
226 City Road
London EC1V 2TT

www.qed-publishing.co.uk

A catalogue record for this book is available from the British Library.

ISBN 978 1 84835 680 1

Printed in China